D0579545

Hungry Monster
ABC

An Alphabet Book

Hungry Monster

WITHDRAWN **ABC**

An Alphabet Book

CONTRA COSTA COUNTY LIBRARY

by Susan Heyboer O'Keefe

Illustrated by **Lynn Munsinger**

LITTLE, BROWN AND COMPANY

New York ⁓ Boston

3 1901 04156 3562

For my son Daniel,
whose ABCs now include TGIF
—S.H.O'K.

For Graydon
—L.M.

Text copyright © 2007 by Susan Heyboer O'Keefe
Illustrations copyright © 2007 by Lynn Munsinger

All rights reserved.

Little, Brown and Company

Hachette Book Group USA
1271 Avenue of the Americas, New York, NY 10020
Visit our Web site at www.lb-kids.com

First Edition: June 2007

Library of Congress Cataloging-in-Publication Data

O'Keefe, Susan Heyboer.
Hungry monster ABC / by Susan Heyboer O'Keefe ; illustrated by Lynn Munsinger. — 1st ed.
p. cm.
Summary: When a child tries to teach the alphabet to ten insatiable monsters, things quickly get out of hand
and chaos abounds until the teacher returns with just the right threat to chase them all away.
ISBN-13: 978-0-316-15574-8
ISBN-10: 0-316-15574-8
[1. Monsters—Fiction. 2. Stories in rhyme. 3. Alphabet.] I. Munsinger, Lynn, ill. II. Title.
PZ8.3.O37Hun 2007
[E]—dc22
2006015422

10 9 8 7 6 5 4 3 2 1

TWP

Printed in Singapore

The illustrations for this book were done in watercolor and ink on watercolor paper.

Book design by Maria Mercado

Ten hungry monsters
visit school today.
They're here to learn the alphabet
the hungry monster way.

"**A** is always apple,"
I tell them from the start.
"**B** is sometimes book
that's filled with lovely art."

"**C** can be for crayon."
  (My favorite color's green.)
"And **D** can be for desk,
  which should be neat and clean."

Hungry monsters eat the fruit
and use the books as stairs
to color on the ceiling,
despite some angry glares.

They do agree my desk should be
all soapy clean and neat,
and so they use it as a tub
to wash their hairy feet.

Then *they* tell *me* "experiment"
should be our word for **E**.
"Excitement" and "explosions"
are so much fun to see.

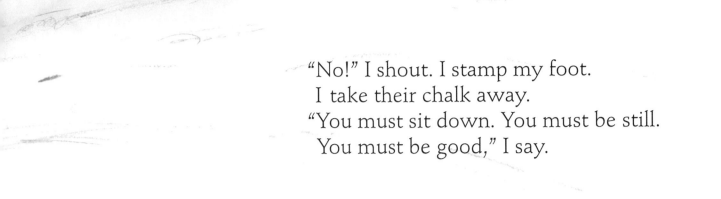

"No!" I shout. I stamp my foot.
 I take their chalk away.
"You must sit down. You must be still.
 You must be good," I say.

"**F** is for a feather
from a falcon's mighty wing.
G is for a grasshopper,
a bug that doesn't sting."

"**H** should be for handkerchief
for when your nose is wet.
I is for iguana,
Ms. Tubbins' classroom pet."

"**J** can be for jumping jacks
at recess or in gym.
And **K** can be a kindly king
who's from the Brothers Grimm."

The monsters tickle both my feet
then set the 'hopper loose.
They tie the hankies on their heads
and serve the lizard juice.

They say that jumping jacks are best
upon a trampoline.
They jump so high to touch the sky
they scarcely can be seen.

And then a brand-new teacher
(the kind that's short and furred)
steps in to finish matching
each letter with a word.

L is always lunchtime
when monsters are around.
They want their grilled cheese sandwiches
with bacon nicely browned.

They hope that **M**'s for mango,
a messy, juicy treat,
because they like to end their meals
with something very sweet.

N should be for napkin
since monsters are polite.
They wipe their sticky horns and tails
with every single bite.

O can be for olives
they didn't see before,
oranges, and onions—
they beg and plead for more.

P is purse or pocketbook
they hope has more than lint,
'cause after-mealtime monster breath
could really use a mint.

"**Q**," I say, "is question
about a book or map.
R should be for rest time."
(Though monsters never nap.)

"**S** is for the many stars
  I get each time I'm good."
I don't think I'll get one today,
although I wish I could.

"**T** is for Ms. Tubbins,
my teacher all year long.
U is for umbrella
for when the weather's wrong."

"**V** is for vacation."
I need to take mine soon—
or better yet, I'd like to send
some monsters to the moon.

"**W**'s for Wiffle ball.
(In gym they'll show you how.)"
But Wiffles aren't waffles.
The monsters know that now.

"**X**, **Y**, **Z**?" I look around.
My palms begin to sweat.
I cannot see a single way
to end the alphabet.

Monsters to the rescue—
they quickly make a call.
Then **X** and **Y** and also **Z**
come tramping down the hall.

X-ray man, a yeti,
a zombie dripping goo—
when you're a hungry monster,
your friends are monsters, too!

"It's time to stop," Ms. Tubbins says,
"and drive out every pest!
Here are words each monster hates:
Homework, *grades*, and *test*!"

Then ten hungry monsters
and monster buddies, too,
jump right out the window but—
Ms. Tubbins grabs my shoe.